About the Book

Rory, Kay and Gerald all agreed. Wheels were more fun than anything. But one day while the three escaped the rain in a night watchman's hut, Rory's scooter and Gerald's racing bike disappeared.

With no clues and a whole town to search, their wheels seemed lost forever. But they thought that, maybe, if they started right back where they lost them. . . That was the beginning of a trail of gypsies, a Rag and Bone man, the milkman's boy, the butcher.

Again, Dorothy Clewes has created an engaging adventure that's fun from start to finish. With Sofia's beguiling illustrations ROLLER SKATES, SCOOTER AND BIKE ranks with the most delightful of the Rory, Kay and Gerald books.

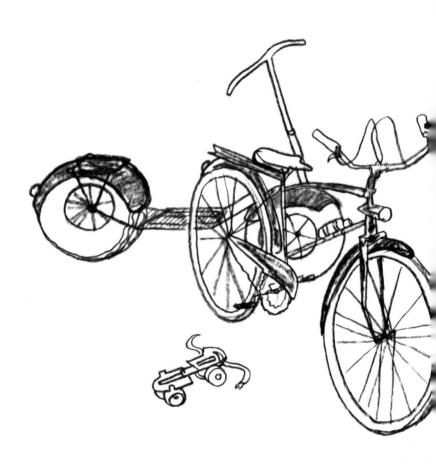

Illustrated by Sofia

ROLLER SKATES, SCOOTER AND BIKE

by DOROTHY CLEWES

Coward-McCann, Inc.   New York

CONTENTS

ROLLER SKATES,
SCOOTER AND BIKE

1

Roller Skates, Scooter and Bike

RORY came flying down the hill on his scooter. Actually it wasn't much of a hill and he wasn't actually flying — but if you bent low over the handlebars and took your foot off the little platform every now and again to push, it felt like flying.

"Mind you only ride on the sidewalk," his mother had said, "and watch you don't bump into anyone."

And so Rory kept his finger on the bell and rang it even when there wasn't anyone in the way

9

because that too made it sound as if he was going faster.

As a matter of fact the sidewalk was empty — until he got to the apartments, and then just ahead of him someone shot out of the entrance: someone he recognized immediately. It was Kay. And Kay was on roller skates. She was standing straight, her ponytail flying out behind her, arms swinging by her side.

"Kay. Kay. Wait for me," Rory called, pushing hard on the pavement, thrusting his scooter forward faster and faster.

Kay stopped as if she had applied an invisible brake and waited for Rory to catch up with her.

"Where are you going?" Rory asked, coming to a standstill beside her.

"Nowhere special," Kay said. "Just around."

"Race me to the end of the road," Rory said. He knew she would win because she had eight wheels against his two, but they were very small wheels and had to go around much faster than his two larger ones did to cover the same amount of ground.

"One, two, three — go!" Kay called, pushing out with one roller-skated foot and bringing up the other one to ride with it, bending slightly forward so that her legs wouldn't shoot out from under her. For a few yards Rory kept even with her, one foot down hard on the little platform of his scooter, hands gripping the handlebars, his other foot pushing down on the pavement — and then Kay started to pull ahead. She reached the end of the pavement and was beginning to slow down so that she wouldn't shoot off into the road, when without the slightest warning, around the corner appeared a bicycle.

To Rory who was coming behind and so saw it all happen it was really very funny. Kay had almost stopped moving because she had come to the corner. The bicycle was going so slowly that it was wobbling anyway, so it was more from sheer surprise than anything else that the rider lost his balance, toppled from the saddle onto Kay and they both, very gently, sank down in a heap onto the ground. But what was even funnier was that underneath the bicycle wheels, the legs and the arms, was Gerald. Gerald was their friend — a bit older than they were but he often played with them when he hadn't anything better to do, which was most of the time.

"Why don't you look where you're going?" Gerald fumed, beginning to untangle himself and feeling very *un*-friendly.

"I like that," Kay stormed. "It was all your fault: bicycles aren't allowed on sidewalks."

"They are today," Gerald said, "because the road's up. Look what you've done to my bike." He pointed to a tiny scratch on the handlebars. "And I wouldn't be surprised if you haven't bent the front wheel." He spun it on its axle, testing it.

"Kay didn't bump into you, you bumped into Kay," Rory said, joining them. "I saw it happen."

"You see," Kay said, picking herself up and brushing herself off. "I've got a witness." She wasn't hurt but as the bicycle had toppled over, one of the pedals had caught her on the knee and now a tiny trickle of blood was beginning to run down her leg. "Look what you've done to my leg," she told him. "I wouldn't be surprised if I don't get blood poisoning and die."

"It isn't anything, it's only a scratch," Gerald said. All the same, the blood made it look as if it really was his fault. "Haven't you got a handkerchief?" he asked her.

"Yes, but it's a clean one," Kay said. "I'll borrow yours."

Gerald's was a clean one, too, but he did not see how he could not lend it and so, reluctantly, he dug into his pocket for it.

Kay dabbed at her knee until Gerald's handkerchief was covered with little red spots and until no more blood would come. Then she folded the handkerchief into a long bandage and wrapped it around the damaged part.

"It ought to be washed and disinfected," Rory said, meaning Kay's knee, because that was what his mother did whenever he fell down and made himself bleed.

"I'll do it when I get home," Kay said. "Let's go and have a look at the road."

2

The Voices

THEY wheeled their way up the road, Rory on his scooter, Kay on her roller skates, and Gerald on his bicycle, which seemed none the worse for its shake-up. A few yards up the road they could see quite clearly the upheaval that had forced Gerald up onto the sidewalk. A long trench had been dug along the road, and at intervals someone had put little scarlet lanterns ready to be lit when it got dark to warn traffic not to fall into the hole.

"What's it going to be?" Rory asked.

15

"I expect someone's going to plant lampposts," Kay said. The road had always been very dark. She had often heard her father say: "Someday there'll be an accident if that road isn't lit properly."

Rory looked down into the deep trench. Already someone had planted empty milk bottles and he couldn't imagine what would grow from them.

"Cows, perhaps," Kay said, because she could never resist teasing Rory.

"Or milk churns," Gerald said, because he always tried to go one better than Kay although he never succeeded.

They followed the trench up the road until it stopped being a trench and became a road again. But that wasn't quite all. Where the trench ended a little hut had been put up: a hut made of dark green canvas stretched over a frame. A green canvas curtain was pulled across the front to make a door.

"It isn't locked and it doesn't say TRESPASSERS WILL BE PROSECUTED," Rory said. Often that was the notice planted outside fields and woods that

16

looked especially inviting. It was another way of saying KEEP OUT.

"It's private property, all the same," Gerald said. His father was a builder and often had to leave bricks and planks of wood outside, but when he did he always covered them over with a tarpaulin which was meant to keep people from touching.

"What's a tarpaulin?" Rory asked. It was a long, unfamiliar word and he had never heard it before.

"It's the same as a canvas sheet," Gerald told him, feeling superior for knowing, "but water-proof, in case it rains — and what's underneath it is private property," he said again.

"Well, we're not going to take anything," Kay assured him. "We're only going to look."

Inside it was a real little house. There was a long bench seat made by resting a plank of wood on two upturned buckets; six bricks arranged close together made a table; and on the table there was a small tin kettle and a tin mug. In front of the bench seat, standing on three little legs, there was a round fire basket full of coals.

"It's a night watchman's hut," Gerald said. "When it's dark some old boy will come along with his supper wrapped up in a red-spotted hand-kerchief, light the fire in the fire basket, and pre-pare to spend the night here."

It had turned dull while they were looking at the little hut and now it began to rain.

"We'd better take shelter until it stops," Kay said, stepping quickly inside, and as the other two hesitated: "Well, it's silly to get wet. No one can say we're doing any harm, we're just taking shelter."

It looked cozy inside the hut and it was raining harder every minute, so Gerald went to lean his bicycle up against a garden wall where a hedge made a little roof over it, and Rory did the same with his scooter. When they got back to the hut Kay was sitting on the bench.

"Pull the curtain and sit down," she said, mak-ing room for them. She had taken the folded makeshift bandage from her knee and spread it out on the brick table like a cloth. Sprinkled over

18

as it was with the blood spots it looked just like a workman's spotted handkerchief—only there was no food wrapped up in it.

"I've got some toffee," Gerald said, diving a hand into his pocket and bringing out a handful of hard candy.

"And I've got a chocolate bar," Rory said, bringing that out of his pocket.

Kay shared the candy bar, and if you didn't think too much about it being chocolate and toffee you could imagine you were eating bread and cheese and perhaps a cold sausage or two. They munched happily for a few moments and then Kay held up a silencing finger. "Listen!"

Now Rory and Gerald could hear the sound, too — the crunch of footsteps on the gravel pathway and voices. The footsteps stopped outside the hut but the voices went on, not clear so that you could understand what was being said, but muffled because of the green canvas tarpaulin, the sound of words mixed with laughing. Kay and Rory and Gerald sat like statues, not breathing, waiting for the canvas curtain to be pulled back and show

them up — but in another moment the crunching footsteps began again and the muffled voices grew fainter and fainter and finally couldn't be heard any more.

"I have to go home now," Kay said, folding up the spotted handkerchief and giving it back to Gerald.

"Me, too," Rory said. His mother had said not to stay out long but at least he hadn't got wet.

"Anyway it's stopped raining now," Gerald said. If it had been the night watchman he couldn't have blamed them for taking shelter, but it was a good idea to go now before he really did come. He turned to retrieve his bicycle from where he had left it under the hedge by the wall, but there was nothing standing there. The bicycle had gone.

3

Kay Goes in Search

"**M**Y scooter's gone, too." The choking lump clutching at Rory's throat could not have been more painful if he had actually swallowed the scooter.

"Your scooter's secondhand," Gerald said. "My bicycle is new."

"It's as good as new," Rory protested. It was true that it had belonged to someone else in the first place. His father had bought it from a friend whose own little boy had grown too big for it. The boy's name — CHARLIE BROOKS — was still there on the underside of the platform you stood on, so you would never know unless you turned the scooter over and looked especially. If ever he got his scooter back again he'd scratch Charlie Brooks' name out and write his own there, Rory told himself.

"Perhaps we can catch them," Gerald said. "They can't have got far." All the time they were standing there talking the scooter and the bicycle were getting farther and farther away, and if whoever had taken the scooter and the bicycle was riding them they would be getting even farther away — but he didn't dare think about that let alone say it aloud.

"You can't catch them but perhaps I can," Kay said. When Gerald and Rory had left their wheels under the shelter of the hedge by the wall she had kept hers on her feet. As a matter of fact since she had had the roller skates she had worn them so much that they had begun to feel like part of her. "You'd better follow me, but if we lose each other we'll meet back at the apartments."

They all started off up the road together but

very soon Kay was a long way ahead. She went so fast that it seemed impossible that she shouldn't catch up with someone, but when she got to the end of the road there was not a soul in sight.

Kay looked one way and then the other. If you went to the right the road took you out to the country. If you went to the left you came back to the town. She considered what she would have done if she'd been with a friend and they'd found a scooter and a bicycle. She would have wanted to get home with it as quickly as possible to show it to all her friends, she decided, and so she turned down the road that led to the houses and the apartments and the shops in the town.

She slowed down when she came to the houses, looking over the gates and the fences, in and out of the entrances of the blocks of apartments, and when she came to the shops she looked carefully in at the doorways of each one to see if a bicycle or a scooter had been left standing there while the owner had gone in to buy something — but the only things that were left waiting outside the shops were baby carriages and dogs. When she arrived

back at her own block of apartments Rory and Gerald were already there.

"You didn't find them." It wasn't a question, but a statement, and the look on Rory's face said plainly that he hadn't really expected that she would.

Gerald said, "You were so long we began to think you'd been stolen, too."

It was the first time the word "stolen" had been mentioned. "Borrowed," Kay had said to herself, and "found," but stolen meant that whoever had taken the scooter and the bicycle did not mean to give them back.

"We'll have to go to the police," Kay said.

It's what they should have done in the first place, Gerald knew that, but police stations were places you only went to if you got into trouble.

"Well, we're in trouble now," Kay said. "Let's go and tell them."

4

Reported Missing

REPORTED missing — a scooter and a bicycle," the policeman said, reaching into his pocket for a pencil. "Where were they taken from?"

"Park Road," Gerald said — and hoped the policeman wouldn't ask him what they had been doing there.

Park Road, the policeman wrote in his notebook. "You live there?" he asked Gerald.

Gerald shook his head.

"We were taking shelter from the rain," Kay

27

said. "When we came out the scooter and the bicycle had gone."

Scooter and bicycle gone, wrote the policeman. "What was the number of the house?"

"It didn't have a number," Kay said quickly. "It was the house where the road repair ends."

"And we'd leaned them against the wall under a hedge so they wouldn't get wet," Rory said, "while we were keeping dry."

"Don't you know that you shouldn't let things like scooters and bicycles out of your sight?" the policeman said, "Unless they're securely padlocked. I don't suppose they were securely padlocked?"

Rory and Gerald shook their heads.

"One scooter's just like any other," the policeman said, "and bicycles are stolen every day. Well, let's have a description. The scooter ...?" He looked across the counter at Rory.

"Red — with yellow wheels," Rory said.

"The same as hundreds of others," the policeman said. "Any identifying mark?"

Rory didn't know what an identifying mark

meant, but he was quite sure his scooter didn't have one.

"And the bicycle?" the policeman said, turning to Gerald.

"Just — a bicycle," Gerald said. Surely everyone knew what a bicycle looked like?

"You're not being smart, are you?" the policeman said. "You know what I mean. Has it got any extras — like a three-speed gear, or a luggage rack, and maybe it's got curved handlebars and flasks to hold drinking water for when you get thirsty on a long ride."

"Yes, of course," Gerald said indignantly. "It's got everything."

Racing-style bicycle, the policeman wrote, and added the question he'd asked Rory. "Any identifying mark?"

It had a number somewhere, Gerald knew that, all bicycles had, and he had been meaning ever since he got the bicycle to write it in his diary but somehow he'd never got around to it.

"They don't put numbers on for fun, you know," the policeman said, "but it's a waste of time, isn't it, if no one's going to take any notice of them? Well" — he scratched his head doubt-fully — "there isn't much to go on, is there — but we'll do our best."

"He isn't going to find them, is he?" Rory said when they got outside, swallowing on the lump in his throat. It was the first scooter he had ever had. It was the first anything he'd had on wheels.

"Of course he is," Kay said. "We've reported them missing. It's his job to find them."

"He'd better," Gerald said, but the policeman hadn't sounded very hopeful although he'd done a lot of writing in his book. And on top of every-thing, he'd have to tell his father and that was al-most worse than losing the bicycle even though he had saved up and paid for it with his own money — well, most of the money had been his own.

"I expect they'll be waiting for you by the time you get home," Kay said. Where Rory and Ger-ald lived had been the last thing the policeman had asked and he wouldn't have done that if he hadn't meant to hand them back himself.

"Call for me in the morning," Kay said, "and we'll do some more racing."

5

The Scene of the Crime

WHEN Kay came out of the apartments next morning Rory and Gerald were sitting on the low wall that ran around the paved area that protected the apartments from the busy road. She could tell at once by the look on their faces that the policeman hadn't found anything.

"Was your father very cross?" she asked Gerald.

"No," Gerald said. And that had been odd now that he came to think about it — his father had been much more angry with the police. "They expect me to pay my taxes and they can't catch a two-bit thief," he had stormed. He had telephoned the police station and told them exactly what he thought about it.

"Mine wasn't either," Rory said. In fact his mother had not been really sorry at all. She hadn't been very happy about him having the scooter in the first place because the roads were so busy and she didn't quite trust him to stay on the sidewalk, but his father had said it was time he grew up and the only way to learn about something was to do it. What his mother was sorry about was that he should have lost something that he liked so much. "If the police don't bring it back," she said, "we'll see what we can find to put in its place." He didn't want anything in its place. All he wanted was the scooter to be his again.

"Let's go where it all began," Kay said. "This time she had left her roller skates behind because it wasn't any fun being on wheels when Rory and Gerald couldn't be.

"All right," Gerald said. It was better to be doing something than sitting thinking about what had happened.

"Perhaps someone was playing a game with us and we'll find them where we left them," Rory said, hopefully.

They ran down the road to where it turned the corner. It all looked exactly the same — the deep trench in the road and the little red lanterns standing guard at intervals all the way up the road until they got to the hut — but then they saw that this time the curtain was drawn back from the entrance to the hut and in front of it the coal bucket glowed.

"There's someone there," Kay said.

"It's the night watchman," Gerald said.

"It's daytime and we've only just had breakfast," Rory said. "It must be the day watchman."

"Very funny," Gerald said. He was quite sure there wasn't such a person as a day watchman, but he wished he'd thought of saying it first.

They followed the little red lanterns up the road. When they got close to the hut they could see that there was a kettle sitting on the hot coals of the fire bucket. Beyond it, inside the hut, sitting on the bench seat they had sat on the day before, was an old man. In one hand he held a loaf of bread and in the other a penknife. On a red-spotted handkerchief spread out in front of him was a wedge of cheese and a slab of butter in its paper wrapping. U.S.1367286

Rory said, "You're the day watchman."

The old man looked up from his meal. "That's right," he said. "Day watchman and night watchman."

"What are you watching?" Kay asked him.

"Property," the old man said, taking a large bite out of the thickly buttered crusty bread. "If things are left about and not watched people start taking a fancy to them."

"Someone took a fancy to something we left here yesterday," Gerald said. "A scooter and a bicycle."

"Ah —" The old man nodded his head knowingly. "So they belonged to you, did they?"

"You found them!" Rory's voice was high-pitched with excitement.

But the old man was shaking his head. "No, no, no, no — but the police, they've been around,

35

asking questions. There wasn't nothing I could tell them. I didn't come on duty till last night and there was nothing here then."

"We came before that to look at the hole," Kay said, "and then it began to rain and so we took shelter in your hut."

"Do something you shouldn't do and no good always comes of it," the old man said.

"And I leaned my bicycle against the wall there." Gerald pointed to the wall with its overhanging hedge.

"And I put my scooter with it," Rory added.

"How was it you couldn't see what was going on, then?" the old man asked them. "No one could take anything from under my nose without my seeing them."

"We'd pulled the curtain across," Kay confessed, "and when we heard the voices we thought it was you and we kept very still and after a little while the voices went away."

"Ah—so you heard voices. What sort of voices?"

Kay had not thought about the voices from that moment to this, but now she was hearing them again. "They were boys' voices," she said.

"Or men's," Gerald said.

"Two — I think," Kay said. It could have been more but if it had been it would have made a bigger sound.

"They were muffled — and giggling," Rory said. He was remembering that he had wondered what they were giggling about; now he knew.

"That doesn't sound like the Rag and Bone man," the day watchman said, "but he's the only one I've seen around here. Folks in the houses put things out for him. Could be he thought the scooter and the bicycle had been put out for him, too."

"Where does he live?" Gerald asked him.

"I'm not saying it is him," the old man said. "I'm only saying I've seen him around, collecting things. He has a yard — back of High Street."

They all knew where that was. It was a lane that had once led to stables where tradesmen kept their horses and vans. The horses and the vans had been gone a long time and now the stables were garages for trucks and cars. The last to go had been the milkman's. He'd kept his pony there before he had the truck.

"We could go and ask him if he'd taken them by mistake," Kay said.

"No harm in doing that," the old man agreed, "but you'd best be quick because he sells things fast."

6

Rags and Bones

IT was quiet in the lane. The garages stood open and empty, cars and trucks taken out on their journeys for the day — but at the end of the lane a cart stood. There was a pony between the shafts. His head was down, his muzzle deep in a sack of oats.

At first they thought the milkman must have gone back to having the milk cart again instead of the truck — but as they got closer a man who certainly wasn't the milkman came out of the stable and began emptying the cart, taking out a

40

carpet, a bundle of lace curtains, a broken lamp-shade. He wore a coat that came down nearly to his ankles, but when he turned around they could see that he wasn't a man at all but a boy, a boy not much older than Gerald.

"I've no toys today," he called to them.

"We don't want toys," Kay said. "We're looking for the Rag and Bone man."

"Well, that's me," the boy said. "If you want me to collect something tell your ma to put it out and I'll pick it up tomorrow morning."

Rory said, "We came to see if you'd picked up something yesterday that wasn't put out for you."

"What do you mean by that now?" Suddenly the boy looked angry.

"He means by mistake," Gerald said hastily. "We left a scooter and a bicycle in Park Road, near the night watchman's hut — while we took shelter from the rain."

"When we came out they'd gone," Kay said.

"Well, you won't find them here," the boy said. "You don't build up a business by taking what doesn't belong to you." He still sounded angry,

but less so. He said in a moment, "You asked for it, though, didn't you? If I left a scooter and a bicycle in the street I'd expect to lose them."

"Who would take them?" Kay asked him.

"Anyone wanting to make a bit of money," the boy said. "Some folks would sell their own grandmothers if they were hard up. Then again it might be someone who'd never had a scooter or a bicycle and couldn't resist helping himself to one for nothing."

Rory could understand that. Before he'd had his scooter he'd often stood in front of Mr. Pringle's shop wishing he could just help himself to one from the glittering rows of bicycles, tricycles, and scooters put outside for show.

"Come to think of it," the boy said, stopping in the middle of lifting a bottomless rocking chair out of his cart. "The house I picked this up from yesterday — there was a scooter lying in the hall there. I remember because I had to move it out of the way or I'd have fallen over it. Yellow with red wheels."

"Mine was red with yellow wheels," Rory said.

"Red with yellow wheels, yellow with red wheels," the boy said. "It could have been either way around."

"Did you see a bicycle as well?" Gerald asked him.

"I didn't see one but that doesn't say there wasn't one there." He carried the rocking chair into the stable and arranged it upside down on the top of a chest of drawers in one corner.

"Can you remember the house?" Kay asked him.

"It was out on the Woodbury road," the boy said. "If you like to hang on till I've emptied the cart I have to go that way again and I'll give you a lift. No harm in looking."

It wouldn't be the same, it couldn't be, Kay thought, but a ride in the pony cart was something that couldn't be missed, and she could tell from the look on the faces of Gerald and Rory that they thought so, too. In fact, they were already helping to empty the cart so they could go more quickly, and so Kay went to help, too. The sack of rags was enormous but it was quite light.

44

"What do you do with all these rags?" she asked the Rag and Bone boy.

"Sell 'em," the boy said. "Everything's worth something. Rags get turned into paper."

"You mean — paper you write on?" Kay could not believe it, looking at the strips of velvet, the scraps of cotton, old woolen jumpers, and knots of nylon stockings.

"To write on, to wrap things up in, to make into books, envelopes, magazines, newspapers. They'll get sorted out and washed and chewed up by a great machine and it'll come out as paper."

"What about the furniture?" Gerald asked. He couldn't see that any of it was worth anything but chopping up for firewood.

"Well — take that rocking chair for instance," the boy said. "I've a pal who'll weave a new cane bottom for that. I'll give it a lick of paint and it'll be as good as new. And I don't always sell," he said. "Sometimes I do an exchange."

"It says Rags *and* Bones," Rory said, reading the words printed around the sides of the cart.

"I don't get so many of those," the boy said, "but when I do they sell for making glue."

45

"You mean the stuff that sticks things?" Rory asked in astonishment. His mother was throwing bones away all the time, after she'd carved the meat off them and after they'd been used to make soup — and when she couldn't find a neighbor's dog to give them to.

"That's right," the Rag and Bone boy said. "It's a good trade, this is. My father had it before me and his father had it before him. I've got a reputation to keep up and I'm not likely to ruin it taking stuff I'm not supposed to." The slur on his character still rankled but he was feeling happier now that he had spoken up for himself. "I didn't get much schooling but I make out all right," he said. "It's mostly profit, too. All I have to pay for is the stable and Old George there."

Old George, hearing his name, lifted his head out of the bag of oats, blew appreciatively through his long nose and tossed his head.

"All right," the Rag and Bone boy said, unhitching the bag and throwing it into the cart, " — ready to go. Get yourselves in and we'll be off."

It wasn't easy getting into the cart although

46

there were two tiny iron footsteps to help you up. To begin with, Old George, refreshed from his meal, refused to stand still, so that the cart wouldn't stay in the same place for two minutes together. However, with the Rag and Bone boy standing at his head, and Kay giving Rory a helpful heave from behind, and Gerald giving Kay a heave, and Gerald — who was really too old to be heaved in by anyone — hauling himself up and into the cart, they managed.

Sitting close together there was room for all of them on the bench seat — not unlike the bench seat in the night watchman's hut, Kay couldn't help thinking, but this was a real seat, not a plank of wood balanced on two upturned buckets.

They clip-clopped up the lane and turned into High Street, the Rag and Bone boy putting a hand out to warn the traffic to slow down and give him right of way.

"Horses always have the right of way," he said, "because they came before cars. It's a rule."

What a lot of things they'd learned today, Kay thought — from a Rag and Bone boy, too, who hadn't had much schooling.

"I reckon if I'd had regular schooling, too," the boy said, "I'd get to be Prime Minister, but this is what I like best, sitting up here in my own cart behind my own horse, doin' what I want in my own time."

All the same it wasn't as good as a scooter, Rory was thinking. You didn't have to stable and feed a scooter, and it stayed still while you got on.

It wasn't as good as a bicycle, either, Gerald was thinking. On a bicycle, if it was a racing-style model, you could go as fast as a horse, and it was easier to park it — though it certainly was easier to lose than a horse would be.

Roller skates were the best of all, Kay was thinking. All you did was fasten them on your feet and forget all about them. That way they were part of you and you couldn't ever lose them.

They rattled along High Street, past the super-market and past the Town Hall and past the school where term would start again next week, and when they got to the end they turned right and rattled along the road that went to Woodbury.

7

False Alarm

"THIS is it," the Rag and Bone Boy said, pulling Old George to a standstill outside a large house. It stood by itself inside a large garden, behind a stone wall.

"We sure got here fast," Rory said, wishing the ride could have gone on a lot longer.

"So we did," the Rag and Bone boy said. "Four wheels and four legs gets you over the ground pretty quick."

Gerald climbed down first and gave a hand to Kay, who gave her hand to Rory.

"Come and see me again," the Rag and Bone

boy called to them. "Let me know if you find the scooter and the bicycle."

They watched him out of sight and then turned to the house. The wall was high — well, higher than Kay and Rory — but Gerald could just see over it standing on tiptoe.

"Is there anyone there?" Rory asked him.

"No, but the windows are open," Gerald told him, "and there's some washing on a line."

"Good," Kay said. "That means they're at home." She had already lifted the latch of the heavy iron gate and was pushing it open.

It was spring but the garden was full of last year's leaves. They covered the flower beds and made a soft rustling sound as Kay and Rory and Gerald kicked their way up the path to the front door. By the side of the door there was a handle on the end of a long, thin rod. Kay put up a hand and pulled it. A long way away a bell rang — rather like the school bell, Kay thought, only it didn't go on ringing so impatiently or so long. Soon after it had stopped they heard footsteps and in a moment the door opened.

The lady looking down at them was not ever so old but she wasn't ever so young, either. When she saw Kay and Rory and Gerald standing there she looked very surprised.

"I was expecting a friend," she explained.

"We're looking for a scooter — " Kay began.

"And a bicycle," Gerald said.

"I don't know anything about a bicycle," the lady said, "but — oh dear, was the scooter yours?"

"A red one with yellow wheels," Rory told her. He couldn't hide his excitement. They'd found it at last, they'd really found it.

"Why, yes, I believe it was. It had been tossed over my wall into the bushes. I remember thinking it was much too good to be thrown away. Now I suppose you're sorry and want it back?"

"Yes, please — and I didn't throw it away," Rory said indignantly. "I left it for a moment and when I went back for it it had gone."

"Oh, dear," the lady said again, and now she looked upset. "I gave it to the Rag and Bone man when he came to collect some other things, but he didn't take it and I gave it away to someone else.

52

Well — you can't blame me for getting rid of it, can you? All my little boys and girls are grown-up and don't live here any more."

"Who did you give it to?" Kay asked.

"A gypsy woman," the lady said. "She came to the door selling baskets of primroses. I didn't want any but she insisted on leaving one just the same — and so I gave her the scooter."

For a basket of primroses! Rory opened his mouth to say something but no sound would come out. The scooter had so nearly been his again, but now it was as far away as ever.

"Do you know which way she went?" Kay asked.

The woman shook her head. "That was yesterday," she said. "Gypsies wander from place to place, you know. By now they could be anywhere at all."

8

The Milkman Makes a Suggestion

"THAT was your scooter, all right," Gerald said, "but what about my bike?" They were standing outside the house, wondering what to do next.

"Perhaps that got thrown away, too," Rory said. It was awful that anyone could have thrown his lovely scooter away, over a wall into dirty old bushes as if it was nothing at all — and then even more awful that someone having found it should have given it away.

"Are you kidding?" Gerald was saying. "That

54

bike's worth a lot of money. More likely it's been sold."

The milk truck came rattling down the road, the same truck that brought butter and milk and eggs to the apartments where Kay and Rory lived and to the house where Gerald lived — the same truck that had taken the place of the milk cart. But the milkman had not changed.

"What about making yourselves useful?" he said, lifting out bottles of milk and cartons of cream. "One pint and one cream for the house, and two pints of milk next door while I go over the road."

Gerald took the milk and the cream through the iron gate and up the pathway to the front door of the house they had just come away from, and Kay and Rory each took a pint to the house next door — only it wasn't a real living-in house, it was a house turned into a shop. Over the gate it said WOODBURY MARKET GARDEN, and inside the garden, instead of being set out with flower beds, was set out with rows and rows of lettuce and radishes and spring onions, and in the windows, ready for roasting, were chickens. There were bowls of eggs there, too, and tomatoes, and jars of honey. When they got back to the truck the milkman was talking to Gerald.

"I just thought you might like to make a bit of pocket money," he was saying. "Saturday and Sunday morning only, so I get a bit of the day to myself. At your age I'd have jumped at it."

"I thought you had someone to help you," Gerald said. A boy about his own age always brought the milk to the door on the weekends. His mother often gave him a slice of bread and jam or a piece of cake. "He looks as if he could do with a good meal — and a few more clothes on his back," she always said.

"He's gone and got himself a real job," the milkman said. "A proper paycheck at the end of the week instead of a few dollars."

Gerald was glad the boy had gotten a job but sorry he was not going to see him any more because often when he was cleaning his bike the boy would stop and speak, admiring the bike, appreciating what a good one it was.

"I clean my bike on weekends," Gerald said. "At least, I did up to yesterday."

"What happened yesterday?" the milkman asked him.

"It got stolen," Gerald said. "My bike and Rory's scooter."

"You don't say?" The milkman looked up from the milk book where he was entering his sales.

"My scooter got found and then lost again," Rory said. Somehow, happening twice made it much worse.

"That's why we're here," Kay explained. "It was thrown over this wall, but before we got here the lady found it and gave it to a gypsy."

"Ah — gypsies," the milkman said. "Itchy fingers, they have. Nothing's safe when they're around, I can tell you that."

"She didn't steal it. The lady gave it to her," Kay reminded him.

"Maybe not," the milkman said, "but it looks like she's got something that doesn't belong to her, doesn't it?"

"Do you think they've got my bike, too?" Gerald asked.

"Like as not," the milkman said. "I'd put my last nickel on it if I was a betting man. It wouldn't be too hard to find out, anyway. A swarm of them moved in the day before yesterday. They've got a camp on the edge of the Common."

"We haven't time to go now," Kay said. They'd been out all morning and it had begun to feel like lunchtime some little while ago.

"We'll go this afternoon," Gerald said. He wouldn't have minded missing lunch if it meant finding the bicycle but he didn't want to go to the gypsy camp on his own.

"All right," Kay said, " — and I'll wear my roller skates so we can all ride back together."

9

Rewards for Information

THEY met by the hut where it had all started. Now, as well as the little red lanterns and the trench, there were long lengths of drainpipes and a lot of men with pickaxes were making the trench even longer. But the old watchman wasn't there. The canvas curtain was drawn across the front of the hut just as it had been when they had first seen it.

"He doesn't need to watch while the men are working," Gerald said.

Any other time Rory would like to have stopped

and watched the men swinging their pickaxes, heaving up great chunks of road — but all their thoughts were on their trip to the gypsy camp to get back the scooter and the bicycle. He'd come and see them again tomorrow.

Gerald wasn't interested in them, either. He was thinking: tomorrow, Saturday, he'd be cleaning his bicycle again, oiling it and polishing it, blowing up the tires and filling the water bottles ready for a trip, wiping away all signs that it had ever belonged, even for a few days, to anyone else.

And this evening, Rory's thoughts ran on, he'd scratch out Charlie Brooks' name from underneath the little platform and in its place he'd write his own in clear, black print; his address, too, so that if ever again it got mislaid it could be sent back to him — like a parcel.

"My father put an advertisement in the paper last night," Gerald told Kay and Rory. "He's offering a reward for anyone who finds my bicycle."

It had looked very impressive. LOST FROM PARK ROAD, BOY'S RACING-STYLE BICYCLE. REWARD.

His address was there, too, and his father's telephone number.

"My father put an advertisement in, too," Rory said — but it had gone in too late to catch the morning edition and it was going to have to wait until tomorrow's paper. REWARD — FOR RETURN OF RED SCOOTER WITH YELLOW WHEELS, TAKEN FROM PARK ROAD, his father had written, adding the address, but no telephone number because they didn't have one.

Kay had never thought of a reward being offered for the return of the scooter and the bicycle. She said, "We'd better get them back first, before anyone reads about it in the paper."

"Gypsies don't read newspapers," Gerald said. "They can't read at all because they've never been to school — and if they could they wouldn't spend money on one."

They set off up the road, Kay on her roller skates, Rory and Gerald trotting to keep up with her. This time when she got to the end of the road she turned to the right, taking the road that led to the Common and eventually to Woodbury. She had to stop after she'd gone a little way down the road for Rory and Gerald to catch up with her, roller skates were so much faster than feet, and she stopped, as it happened, exactly outside the house they had visited that morning.

Waiting for Rory and Gerald to catch up with her, Kay went to look through the iron gate into the garden. She had expected it to look empty as it had looked before, but to her surprise the lady was there, just behind the wall, sweeping up the dead leaves.

"Why — if it isn't the little girl who came looking for the scooter," she said, leaving her work for a moment and coming to the gate to speak to Kay. "I've been thinking about you such a lot. Did you find the scooter? I felt so bad about it, giving it away like that."

Kay shook her head. "We're still looking for it," she said.

Gerald and Rory came puffing up, red in the face, out of breath, and looking very hot.

"Oh, how hot and tired you look," the lady

said. "Come inside a moment and I'll bring you a cool drink."

A garden seat and a garden table stood on the lawn and Rory especially was glad to sit down and rest his legs which were so much shorter than Gerald's and which had worked so much harder than Kay's. In a moment the lady came out carrying a tray filled with glasses, a package of biscuits, and a jug of lemonade.

She said, "After you'd gone I was so worried about the scooter that I put an advertisement in the paper. I offered a reward for anyone who would bring it back."

"That makes three rewards," Kay said. "Gerald's father put one in and so did Rory's."

"I put in two advertisements," the lady said. "One for the scooter and another for a gardener. I've got a lot of garden and no one to help me with it."

"We'd stay and help you if we didn't have to find the bicycle and the scooter," Kay told her. It would have been fun brushing up the leaves into a big pile and turning them into a bonfire, digging

out the weeds and smoothing the brown earth around the new spring clumps of daffodils and tulips — and drinks like this when they rested in between.

"I think I really need someone a little older," the lady said, "but it is kind of you to offer."

"We have to go now," Kay said. "Thank you for the lemonade — "

"And for the biscuits," Rory said.

"And if we find a gardener as well as the scooter we'll let you know," Kay said.

10

The Gypsy Camp

THEY soon came to the Common and at first it didn't seem as if there was anyone there but the usual kind of people — a few boys throwing a football about, someone flying a kite, and several ladies giving their dogs a run — but at the far end, where the grass stopped being grass and became bushes and trees, a faint blue film of smoke crept out onto the field.

They walked across the stubbly grass, Kay lifting first one roller-skated foot and then the other so that she looked like a strolling stork, and now as they got closer they could see ponies grazing by the wood, hobbled to stakes in the ground so that they couldn't wander too far away. And through the trees they could see what looked like bright flags waving, and little gaily colored houses standing on wheels and with steps going up to the front doors.

"It's like a little town," Rory whispered. There was no one to hear him except Kay and Gerald, but it seemed safer to speak quietly.

They could hear voices, too. Shouting, laughing voices of boys and girls and the deeper voices of men and women. And singing. And a delicious smell was drifting out from the little wood along with the soft blue smoke —

"You looking for someone?"

The voice startled them so that they spun around. A barefoot boy in a ragged blue shirt tucked into torn gray flannel trousers was coming up behind them, almost as if he'd been stalking them. He was about Gerald's age but thinner, his hair tousled, his face unwashed.

"Yes," Kay said, "we're looking for the lady who had a scooter given to her yesterday."

"Red — with yellow wheels," Rory added.

"She was selling baskets of primroses," Gerald said.

"That sounds like my ma," the boy said, "but she didn't bring no scooter back with her."

"But the lady at the house gave it to her — in exchange for the primroses," Kay said.

"She found the scooter in her garden and thought it had been thrown there by someone who didn't want it any more," Gerald explained.

"But it belongs to me," Rory said. He looked at the boy's hands to see if his fingers looked itchy as the milkman had said — but they didn't look any different from his own.

"You'd better come and ask her yourself," the boy said, and led the way toward the camp. As they passed, the ponies lifted their heads inquiringly, walked with them a little way, and then coming to the end of their tether, lost interest and stooped to their grazing again.

It was like a different world, a picture-book world, Kay thought. The caravans stood in a ring around a crackling fire. Over the fire, slung from an iron chain fastened to a pyramid of three iron rods, hung the pot from which the delicious smell was coming. The laughing boys and girls were playing tag around the fire and around the caravans, and some grown-ups were sitting on the caravan steps and some were hanging out the brightly colored clothes that had looked like flags waving, and others were chopping wood and weaving little baskets from rough wood and string. All were as busy as bees in a hive.

When Rory and Kay and Gerald appeared they all stopped what they were doing — until the boy held up his hand in a kind of sign, as if he were saying: These three are all right. They're my friends. He led them over to the center caravan, the largest and the gayest-painted of them. A woman was sitting on the steps, a big woman with jet-black hair. A shawl served as a blouse, crisscrossed over her front with the ends tucked into a patchwork skirt.

"Well, son?" she said, giving the boy a deep, searching look.

"They want to speak to you," the boy said.

"They say you've got a scooter belonging to the small one."

Rory had never thought of himself as "small," but the way the gypsy boy said it made him sound special.

Kay thought it was like being presented to a queen. As a matter of fact the jet-black hair was braided into a kind of coronet and sat on top of the woman's head just like a crown, and she held herself in a proud way that reduced even Kay to silence for at least two moments.

Gerald thought it looked exactly the kind of place where you'd find a lost scooter — or a lost bicycle — or a lost anything else anyone was stupid enough to leave about, but at least they all seemed friendly. It ought not to be too difficult to persuade them to hand them back.

"I had a scooter given to me yesterday," the woman said. "A red scooter with yellow wheels."

"That's it." Rory was nodding his head excitedly. "That's my scooter. The milkman said we'd find it here."

But the woman with the braided crown on top

of her head was shaking it. "What use would I have for a scooter?" she said, jerking her head in the direction of the squealing, chasing boys and girls. "They've grown out of scooters and the small ones aren't ready for them yet. I sold it for a few dollars. It bought meat for the pot."

"Who bought it?" Rory asked her. It wasn't possible that he'd been so close to getting it back only to find it gone again.

"The man in the shop," the woman said. "He'd a little boy who'd be glad to have it, he said."

"And what about the bicycle?" Gerald said. He had to admit that what the woman had said about the scooter did sound like the truth. The boys and girls running in and out among the washing and hiding under the caravans certainly looked too old for scooters — but any one of them was the right age for a bicycle.

"What bicycle?" A strange, closed-up look had come over the woman's face.

"*My* bicycle," Gerald said. "It was with Rory's scooter. They were both taken while we were sheltering from the rain." They knew something, there was no doubt at all about that.

"You're not saying we stole it, are you?" Up to a moment ago the gypsy boy had been friendly, but now he was looking angry, his head thrust forward, his hands curled into fists.

Gerald shook his head, quaking a bit at the knees, but holding his ground. "I didn't say 'stolen,' I said 'taken,' " he told the boy.

"So what's the difference?" the boy said, insolently.

"You can take something by mistake," Gerald said, "or have it given to you — like the scooter. If you lost your bike wouldn't you want it back?"

And that did it. Suddenly the boy went very red in the face, his hands stopped being fists and he was stuffing them deep into his trouser pockets as if hiding them as well as the bicycle. There wasn't any mistaking the way he looked. He couldn't have looked more guilty if he'd helped himself to the Crown Jewels.

"You *have* got it!" Gerald exploded. "Well, you can jolly well hand it over. Of all the rotten things to do, taking someone's bike."

"He didn't steal it," the woman said fiercely.

"Left to rot, it was — on a junk heap outside the town. People who can't look after their things deserve to lose them."

It was clear now what had happened. Whoever had taken the scooter and the bicycle had got frightened. They'd thrown Rory's scooter over the wall into the lady's garden and tossed his bike on the junk heap. He never would have looked for it there, neither would the police. Well, he'd been lucky, he'd got it back, and in future he'd make sure he never left it again without padlocks all over it.

But the boy wasn't moving. He stood there stubbornly, not looking at anyone, just staring into the grass at his feet.

"All right," the woman said, "let him have it back."

11

Ma Uses Her Powers

THERE was an awful stillness in the camp. The boys and girls had stopped playing and were drawn together watching the three strangers and the big boy who was their brother, or their cousin, or perhaps some more distant relation. The men had stopped weaving their baskets and the women had left their chores of washing and cooking and hanging out the clothes. Even the woman with the crown of hair had got to her feet, not moving, but just standing there, not saying anything more, but willing the boy to do as he'd been told.

"Come on, then," the boy said at last, and turning on his heel led them past the fire with its bubbling cooking pot, to the back of the camp where a tent had been rigged up to store sacks of potatoes, two or three tipsy prams, several broken chairs — and a bicycle.

Gerald stared at it in amazement. It was upside down, standing on its handlebars, both inner tubes were hanging out of the tires, limp and airless, and it was coated over with thick red rust.

"But — that isn't it!" Gerald gasped. The heap of old iron might once have been a bicycle but that must have been a long, long time ago. "Mine's a racing-style bike — with a three-speed gear — and flasks for holding drinking water — and a carrier for parcels — " He was going to say a lot more, but suddenly he had caught sight of the boy's face. It was all at once lit up with delight.

"I — I can keep it, then? It's still mine."

"No one's going to take that from you." Gerald could have made the words sound full of ridicule and disgust, but the way he spoke them even Rory could tell that he meant them as a plain statement of fact. The old bicycle couldn't have meant more to the boy if it had come straight out of Mr. Pringle's shop, mint new — and for once Gerald appreciated the way he felt.

"You should just have seen it when I found it." The boy was bubbling over with enthusiasm now, pointing out to Gerald the length of frame he'd already worked on with emery paper and polish.

"I could give you a couple of tires better than those," Gerald said, examining them. He'd discarded two soon after he bought the bike because he'd wanted racing treads; they were almost new.

"You could?" The boy's eyes were shining.

"I might be able to find an inner tube, too." The burst of generosity had gone to Gerald's head and the feeling was pleasant.

Kay stared at him in amazement. Gerald sold things, or exchanged things. She'd never known him to give anything away before.

"Cross-your-heart?" the boy said. He couldn't really believe what his ears were hearing.

"Cross-my-heart I'll bring them tomorrow," Gerald promised him.

"I'm sorry about your bike," the boy said, as if the two had been comparable. "I hope you find it."

"I hope so, too," Gerald said. Seeing such an old bike in place of the new one he had been expecting to see, and being suddenly confronted by the boy's evident joy over such a wreck, had made his own disappointment slip momentarily into the background, but now it was back again.

Around the campfire the gypsies were waiting, silently — but when they saw the children come back without the bicycle their faces broke into smiles and they started laughing and chattering and working again.

"Perhaps Ma can tell you where it is," the boy said. "She has powers."

"You mean, she can *see* where it is?" Kay was remembering a visit they had paid once to a fair. There'd been a fortune-teller there and she'd been able to tell them things.

"Usually I can't see anything till I've had my palm crossed with silver," Ma said, wiping both palms on her patchwork skirt, "but sometimes I make exceptions."

Gerald held out his hand. It was a bit rusty and greasy where he'd handled the bike but the woman didn't seem to mind. She took it in both hers and gazed at it for what seemed to Kay to be forever and then she said:

"You get it back — and no harm done. I see a good lad here, not a thief. There's a disappointment, too — and then a gladness. That's all," she said, giving Gerald his hand back. "It isn't stolen and you get it back again — and you make a good friend into the bargain."

"Can you tell me — about the scooter?" Rory was holding out his hand.

"Someone should look at my palm," the woman said, "and tell me what an old fool I am. All right, let's see what it's got to tell me."

She took Rory's hand, as she had taken Gerald's, in both of hers and gazed deeply into it. Rory, watching her, couldn't imagine how she could see anything at all because her eyes seemed to be fast closed, but in a moment she opened them wide and looked him straight in the face.

"Are you playing a joke on me?" she said.

Rory shook his head. He couldn't imagine what she could mean.

"You've got it back," she said. "What more do you expect me to tell you?" She pushed his hand away from her.

"But I haven't, really I haven't," Rory assured her. "Please look again." His hand was dirty, too — perhaps she hadn't been able to see properly. He rubbed it on the seat of his trousers and held it out to her once more, but she wouldn't take it.

"It's back with its owner," she said. "A red scooter with yellow wheels — the same one the lady gave me. I saw it clear and don't tell me I've made a mistake. I've had the power to see things before I could walk or talk, and my ma before me and her ma before her."

"It's true," the boy said. "If Ma saw it it's back where it belongs. She don't ever make a mistake."

The policeman must have found it then, Rory decided. He'd get home and there it would be. He wished he had some silver to cross Ma's palm with to show how grateful he was just being told, but he'd changed the dime he'd had for the chocolate bar they'd eaten in the night watchman's hut and he only had a nickel left and that had to last him to the end of the week.

The boy walked with them to where the camp ended and the field began.

"What's in the pot?" Kay asked. The air was full of the richness of it, a deep, satisfying smell that made her wish she was going home to supper instead of tea.

"Sometimes it's rabbit," the boy said, "and sometimes it's squirrel, and again it could be hedgehog — with mushrooms and nettles and maybe a sugar beet that's got left behind when the farmer's gone over the field." He took a deep sniff. "Today it's meat, butcher's meat."

Rory wished Kay hadn't asked so he never would have known about gypsies eating squirrels and hedgehogs.

"It's no different from your eating cows and sheep and pigs," the boy said, "and chickens, and turkey at Christmas."

"I won't eat them again, ever," Rory promised.

"Oh, yes, you will," the boy said. "Man is a carnivorous animal. That means it's natural for him to eat flesh. I learned that at school," he said proudly.

Gerald said, "I didn't know gypsies went to school."

"They do now," the boy said. "It's the law. I bet I've been to more schools than you'll ever see. Each time we pitch camp in a new town I go to a new school. Ma says we'll soon all be living in houses, just like everyone else, but I hope it won't be in my time. I like it best the way it is."

"I wish I was a gypsy," Rory said as they hurried back to the town. He'd forgotten already about their eating squirrels and hedgehogs and nettles and sugar beets, he could only think how exciting it would be sleeping in one of the little houses on wheels, and eating meals in the open around a blazing campfire, and moving on again to the next place when you'd got tired of the one you were in.

"I bet it's nonsense about your scooter, all the same," Gerald said. And if it was nonsense about Rory's scooter it was nonsense about his bicycle coming back and no harm done.

Kay was skating slowly because that way they

could talk. "We don't know for certain till Rory's been home," she said. "We didn't think the fortune-teller at the fair was right, but it all came true in the end." perhaps gypsies' promises were the same, perhaps what they said wasn't quite the way it sounded. "But we'll go on looking just the same — just in case what she said doesn't come true." It wasn't her scooter, and it wasn't her bicycle, but they were having fun looking for them and she didn't want it to end just yet.

12

The Butcher

THEY ran all the way back to the apartments — except Kay who got there first because she was on wheels. She was very tempted to knock on the door and ask Rory's mother about the scooter, but it wouldn't have been fair to spoil Rory's surprise, and so she waited for them to catch up with her.

Rory burst in so excitedly that his mother spun around in alarm thinking something terrible must have happened. When she heard what all the excitement was about she was at first relieved and then disappointed for Rory all over again.

"No one's been here with any scooter," she told him, "and I've been in all day. They couldn't have knocked without my hearing them."

"We're wasting our time," Gerald said. "They're in another town by now. Perhaps they're in another country." He decided there and then that he wouldn't tell his father he'd been to the gypsy camp and had half believed what the woman had told them. And he did partly believe her. He was sure it was true that the woman had sold the scooter, and he knew it was true that the boy hadn't taken his bicycle, but he'd been right about it being nonsense that she could see what had happened. All the same he was going to keep his word to the boy and take him the tires and the inner tubes — even though with new tires *and* new tubes he couldn't imagine that old rusty bike would ever be much good.

Rory's mother didn't really believe, either, that they were ever going to see the scooter again even if Gerald found his bicycle, but she thought it better for Rory to go on looking until he realized this for himself, so she gave them all a glass of milk and a slice of cake and they went chasing off again.

"Going to the gypsy camp was a wild-goose chase," Gerald said as they stood outside the apartments, planning what they would do next. "We didn't learn anything, except that they didn't have them — and that the woman had sold the scooter for a few dollars."

"Well, that's something, isn't it?" Kay said. "She sold it to a man in a shop — " She was remembering and trying to get the words exactly right. "It bought meat — for the pot. That's what she said." She looked at Gerald triumphantly.

"I don't see what there is to get excited about," Gerald said. "There are just about a million shops in the town. It could have been any one of them."

"But — don't you see?" Kay said. "She bought meat for the pot — so it must have been a butcher's shop."

It didn't have to be, it could have been a customer in a butcher's shop, but Gerald had to admit Kay might be right. Anyway, it was worth trying. At least they could call at butchers' shops first.

It was surprising how many butchers' shops

there were in High Street. Kay and Rory and Gerald worked their way up both sides of the street and got the same answer from all of them — No. Until they came to the one right at the end, the one nearest to the road that led to Woodbury and the house where the lady lived who had given the gypsy the scooter.

"Come to think of it — yes," the butcher said, resting his long, sharp carving knife on the counter in front of him. "I had a gypsy in the shop only yesterday."

They ought to have known that she would have come to the nearest butcher's shop, Kay scolded herself. They had started at the wrong end of High Street, but it didn't matter, they'd found the right shop now. "Did she buy meat for the pot?" Kay asked the butcher.

"I don't know about any pot," the butcher said, "but she bought meat, all right — but not for money."

"She bought it in exchange for a scooter," Gerald prompted him.

"Red — with yellow wheels," Rory jumped in with.

"Aye — red with yellow wheels," the butcher said, and then, suddenly wondering how it was they knew so much, "What do you know about it?"

"It was my scooter," Rory said.

"Now, look here," the butcher said. "Your name isn't Charlie Brooks, is it?"

Rory shook his head and tried to speak again but the butcher wouldn't give him a chance. "Well, Charlie Brooks' name was on that scooter. It identified it. And I know Charlie. He's the baker's lad."

It was what the policeman had talked about — a mark that proved it was yours; only because he had left Charlie's name on proved that it was his.

"Under the platform bit you stand on," the butcher said, "the writing as plain as the nose on your face: CHARLIE BROOKS. It's lucky I know his dad."

"It doesn't belong to Charlie any more, though," Rory explained. "My father bought it from his father. He'd grown too big for it. I meant to scratch his name off and put mine there — but I kept forgetting."

"More things are lost that way," the butcher said, shaking his head. "I need my head examined, trusting gypsies. I should have known they don't come by anything honestly."

"Oh — but that isn't true," Kay rushed to their defense. "The lady at the house gave her the scooter. She told us so herself. She'd meant to give it to the Rag and Bone boy but he didn't take it and so the gypsy did."

"You bet she did," the butcher said. "That was a nice scooter, in good condition. And my youngster had been hankering after one. It was just the job — and in exchange for a few dollars' worth of meat." He stopped in the middle of his own angry thoughts and then said, "I've only myself to blame, thinking I could get something for nothing. There isn't any more I can tell you. I took it back to its rightful owner. There wasn't anyone at home so I popped it inside the tool shed at the back. I meant to ring Mr. Brooks" — he shrugged his shoulders, apologetically — "but I haven't had a moment to myself since."

And even now behind Rory and Kay and Gerald the shop was filling, customers coughing and clearing their throats impatiently, tapping their toes on the sawdust-covered floor.

"You must sort it out between you," the butcher said as they edged away from the counter. "All I know is I'd no rights to someone else's property. And now, madam — " He turned to beam at his next customer. "I'm sorry you've been kept waiting. What can I do for you?"

13

The Baker

IT wasn't far to the baker's. They'd passed it only a few moments ago on their way to the butcher's. The lovely smell of newly baked bread met them before they got to the shop and went along with them getting sweeter and more hungry-making all the way. It made Rory swallow hard as if he'd already got a curranty bun in his mouth. It made Gerald reach into his pocket to see how much he'd got to spend if there was anything he couldn't resist, and it made Kay glad she'd still got all her week's pocket money untouched.

BROOKS — BAKER, it said in large letters above the shop window, and in small letters underneath: WEDDINGS AND PARTIES CATERED FOR.

"I expect he'll think we're three customers," Kay said as she lifted the latch and set the bell ringing over the door.

If Mr. Brooks was disappointed to see three small customers standing in his shop instead of three large ones, he didn't show it.

"One currant bun, one chocolate eclair, and one piece of brandy snap," he said brightly, because this was what Rory and Gerald and Kay usually asked for.

But Kay was shaking her head. "We haven't come to buy anything — not first, anyway," she said.

"I'm no good at guessing games," Mr. Brooks said, "never was. How's that scooter, young Rory? Behaving itself, I hope? No wheels off, no screws missing, eh?"

"It's the scooter we've come about," Gerald said.

"I was only joking," Mr. Brooks said. "There couldn't be anything wrong with that scooter. As good as new it was, not a scratch on the paint, even."

"Rory lost it," Kay explained. "And then it got found and lost again — "

" — and after that the butcher bought it," Gerald added.

"— in exchange for meat for the pot," Rory said.

" — but when he turned it upside down it had Charlie's name on it," Kay said.

"— and so he brought it back to you," Rory ended.

"Well, bless my soul," the baker said, "that's a tale and a half, that is, and I'm very sorry to tell you it isn't true. I can't help you. I haven't seen the butcher since I went to pay him my last account. He knows that as well as I do."

"He brought it back but you weren't in," Kay explained. "He said he popped it into the tool shed at the back."

"Well, at least that's something we can see for ourselves," Mr. Brooks said. "You'd better come with me then you'll see the truth of what I'm telling you."

They followed Mr. Brooks around to the back of the counter and through a door. It didn't lead into the tool shed, but as they should have expected, into a huge kitchen. Enormous ovens like cupboards filled the walls, and the largest table Rory had ever seen stood in the middle of the floor. It held wire baskets filled with crusty brown loaves; round and square and oblong with some braided, and some rolled, and some twisted. And wire trays packed with sponge cakes and fruit cakes, cherry cakes and chocolate cakes, buns and crumpets and tarts and biscuits. Rory would like to have lingered but Mr. Brooks was already holding open another door, and this, surprisingly, led into a sitting room just like an ordinary house.

"Well, where do you think I lived?" the baker asked him. "In a flour barrel, I wouldn't be surprised."

Kay hadn't been thinking about it, but now she agreed at once that she wouldn't really have been surprised because the baker did look as if he lived in a flour barrel. A dusting of flour hung like powder to the little hairs on his bare arms and had

settled on his dark hair, turning it to gray. It clung to his eyebrows, too, and rose from his white apron in a little cloud when he slapped his hand against it before he took hold of the knob to open the sitting-room door.

This time they followed Mr. Brooks into a corridor, down the corridor and past where Mr. Brooks kept his hat and coat and walking stick, through yet another door and into a cobbled yard piled high with packing cases and cartons and empty flour barrels. At the end of the yard, almost hidden from sight of the house because of all Mr. Brooks' litter and trash, was the tool shed.

There was a keyhole but no key in it, Gerald couldn't help noticing. Somebody ought to tell Mr. Brooks about padlocks. An unlocked tool shed at the bottom of a yard where you could hardly see it was almost as good a place to get things lost from as a wall under a hedge — but when Mr. Brooks flung open the shed door, there was the scooter.

It was almost as if he was dreaming, Rory thought. Or rather, it was as if all that had happened since he had lost the scooter had been the dream and only this moment was real. There was the scooter, its paint bright red and yellow as if it had never been thrown over a garden wall, or kicked out of the way of a Rag and Bone boy, or dragged down the road into the town by a gypsy.

"Well — what d'you know?" Mr. Brooks exclaimed. "It could have stayed there until it grew whiskers for all I'd ever have known. I never use the shed these days. Can't get to it with all this clutter. There ought to be someone who could move it for me." Me made a halfhearted attempt to push some of it farther against the wall. "The suppliers are always saying they'll take these back but they never come for them. They just bring more."

"The Rag and Bone boy would collect them," Kay said. "He says everything's worth something to someone."

"Now that sounds a smart boy," the baker said. "If you see him you can tell him from me that he can have any of this junk — or all of it. I need space so bad I'll pay him to take it."

Rory was trying out the scooter, balancing on the little platform, wobbling his way back to the house door between the cases and the cartons and the barrels.

"None the worse for its adventure, I hope," Mr. Brooks said, shepherding them back into the shop.

There was a scratch here and there when he came to look closer but he didn't mind them. As a matter of fact, they were a kind of record of all that had happened. He never would try to polish them away.

"Let's say the bun and the eclair and the brandy snap are on the house, shall we?" Mr. Brooks said, stretching out his floury hand and taking one from each of their respective trays.

Kay and Rory and Gerald stood outside eating them, marveling at the return of the scooter.

"D'you know what?" Kay said, in a moment. "The gypsy was right, after all. Your scooter *was* back with its owner — because Charlie Brooks' name was still on it. She wasn't to know it had become yours because you hadn't put your own name there instead."

"It's the first thing I'll do when I get home," Rory said. His name *and* address because next time — if ever it did get lost again — it might not get to someone who knew him the same way the butcher had known Charlie.

"She said I was going to get my bike back," Gerald said, beginning to feel a bit more hopeful.

"Well — you have had the disappointment," Kay reminded him. Nothing could have been more disappointing than to be expecting to see a shiny new bicycle and then have it turn out to be a rusty old thing from off a junk heap. It was all turning out just like the promises made by the fortune-teller at the fair. It would work out right in the end, she was sure. "You've got the gladness to come," Kay said.

14

The Candlestick Maker

"YOU can borrow one of my roller skates if you like," Kay told Gerald, steadying herself by the wall while she unstrapped it from one foot. She'd been lucky not losing her skates — though it would be difficult, she thought, for anyone to take them without taking her, too. Now that Rory had his scooter back it seemed unfair that Gerald shouldn't be on wheels, too.

"Thanks," Gerald said. He'd been wanting to ask Kay for a go on the skates. He fancied himself flying along as straight and as fast as she did, but he'd have liked to have had some practice first.

They spun down the road, Rory on his scooter, Kay sailing along straight as an arrow and as fast, and Gerald very wobbly on the one roller skate that he wasn't used to. Rory and Kay sped past the chandler's shop that stood at the corner of High Street, but immediately began to slow down ready to turn the corner so they wouldn't go onto the road. Gerald would have sped safely past, too — but at that moment someone came out of the shop pushing a pile of sacks on a cart. Gerald wobbled madly, both arms gyrating like the sails of a windmill. There was a *bonk*, a *screech*, and then a *kerplonk* — and Gerald was sitting on the pavement, the wheels of his skate spinning in the air, a sack on his chest, the cart upside down, and someone spread-eagled on the pavement beside him.

Gerald blinked the stars out of his eyes and looked up. He wasn't hurt, thanks to the sacks, only dazed so that for a second he thought he must have bumped into the milkman's truck because the face that was looking into his was the face belonging to the milkman's boy.

There were stars dancing in front of the boy's eyes, too, but through them he recognized Gerald. "Bicycles aren't allowed on pavements," he stormed. "You can be prosecuted; you ought to know that."

"I'm not on a bicycle, I'm on a skate," Gerald told him, holding up a roller-skated foot to prove it. Surprisingly, too, it seemed to be all in one piece.

"Oh." The boy scrambled to his feet now and helped Gerald to his. He never thought about Gerald without thinking about the super bicycle he had — racing style, with three-speed gear, and a carrier, and flasks to hold drinking water for when you went on a long trip. He'd dreamed of having one just like it but never for one moment thought he would ever be able to save up enough to buy one, so that now he couldn't wait to tell Gerald about the wonderful stroke of luck he'd had.

"I've got one," he burst out, so full of his own thoughts that he was sure Gerald must know what he was thinking, too.

"Got what?" Gerald said, dusting himself

down and helping to rearrange the sacks back on the cart.

"I've got one just like yours," the boy burbled on. "A bicycle — racing style, three-speed gear, carrier, drinking bottles — the lot. Come and have a look at it, it's in the yard at the back of the shop. It's how I got this job. ONLY BOY WITH BICYCLE NEED APPLY, the advertisement said — and I'd just got it. You can call that a bit of luck, can't you?"

Gerald wasn't really all that interested. He was more keen to catch up with Kay and Rory and get on with finding his own lost bicycle, but he liked the milkman's boy and felt he owed him something in return for all the admiration and enthusiasm the boy always showed for his own bicycle — even to getting one like it. Imitation, his mother would have said, is the sincerest form of flattery.

The boy tipped the cart of sacks up against the truck he was going to load them into and led Gerald down the yard to where a brightly shining bicycle stood in a slotted wooden stand. He pulled it out, wheeled it around like a prize racehorse, and brought it to a standstill in front of Gerald.

Gerald opened his mouth once, and then twice

before words would come, and then he burst out. "What do you mean, a bicycle like mine? It *is* mine"

"You've found it!" Kay cried, clattering over the cobbles of the yard with Rory to join him. "Oh, I knew we'd find it."

But the milkman's boy was looking furious. "How can it be yours when you've got one?" he cried, snatching the bicycle away so that he was now standing between it and Gerald — and Kay and Rory who seemed to be siding with him.

"Mine was stolen — yesterday," Gerald told him. "We've been looking for it ever since. The police are looking for it, too."

The word "police" took most of the fury out of the boy's voice — but not all of it. "Identify it, then," he said. "It's got a number, you tell me what it is."

It *was* his bicycle, Gerald knew that as if it was part of him, his own flesh and blood — but if anyone had offered him ten bicycles he couldn't have told them the number, and without that he wasn't going to be able to prove it.

And then Kay was speaking, fast as if it was hard to get the words out quickly enough. "We don't know the number — but it has got an identification mark. I bumped into Gerald the way he bumped into you and my roller skates left a scratch on the handlebar — just about where you're holding it."

She couldn't have seen it because the boy's hand was covering it completely — and when he moved his hand, there it was: a tiny, but quite deep scratch, just the kind of scratch a roller skate would make if it bumped into a handlebar.

He wheeled the bicycle over to Gerald. "I bought it yesterday, from a boy who'd bought himself a motorcycle. He let me have it cheap — "

The amount he'd paid was so absurdly small for such a magnificent bicycle that his voice couldn't go on speaking. He'd known, deep down inside himself, that it was much too little to pay for it — even secondhand — although it was plenty for him because it was all he'd had. He should have listened, he knew now, to the little voice that had spoken inside him, telling him to have nothing to do with the deal, just in case —

"I'm sorry," Gerald said. He felt rotten, taking it, as if he was taking something that really did belong to the boy. "What about the job?" he asked him.

The boy shook his head miserably. He'd have to go back to being the milkman's boy a bit longer, until he'd saved up enough to really buy a bicycle — perhaps not a racing-style one with three-speed gear, and carrier, and flasks for holding drinking water, but as long as it would carry him on errands for the chandler it would do.

"There're the rewards," Kay said into the silence.

Gerald and Rory looked at her in amazement.

"Well, we found the scooter and the bicycle, so we're entitled to the rewards. Well, we are, aren't we?"

If anyone else but Kay had asked the question Gerald would have said No, but you didn't argue with Kay. In any case, strictly speaking, she was right. He didn't know what the rewards would amount to, except that he knew his father had it in mind to give five dollars —

"And mine said three dollars," Rory said.

"And the lady wouldn't give less, not living in

a great house like that," Kay said, "and not when she gave the scooter away as if it were her own."

"Even so it won't come to as much as a bicycle will cost," Gerald told the boy, "but it'll help."

"I get a paycheck now," the boy said. "I'd soon save up the rest of it." All the misery had gone and excitement was beginning to bubble up inside him. He was going to be able to keep his job and there was plenty of time to save up for a bicycle like Gerald's — which was much too good, anyway, to use for a job of work.

"I'll pay you back, though," he called after them.

15

Rewards

"THE reward!" Gerald's father spluttered, "but — you found it yourself." All the same, the boy was smarter than he gave him credit for. He'd enjoy telling his friends the story — and made a note in his mind to call the police again and tell them what he thought about them all over again.

"We don't want it for ourselves," Kay said. "It's for the milkman's boy so that he can keep his job which he'll lose now he hasn't got a bicycle."

Gerald's father began to say, What had that got to do with it, for heaven's sake? and then decided it was much less exhausting just to pay the five dollars he'd had in mind to pay as a reward and let it go at that. In any case, he had a kind of a feeling that Gerald might not have found the bicycle without the help — or interference — of Kay.

"The reward!" Rory's father laughed — and knew without having to think twice that Rory certainly would never have thought of *that* for himself, and more than likely would never have found the scooter, either, without the help of Gerald and Kay. Kay, anyway. They'd really worked at it, he had to say that for them. They deserved the reward — and because he didn't have three ones in his pocket, made it five dollars.

"The reward!" The lady had seen them coming up the drive to the house — Gerald on his bicycle, Kay on her roller skates, and Rory on the scooter, the scooter she had found in her bushes, put out for the Rag and Bone boy who hadn't taken it, and then given to the gypsy woman in exchange for a basket of primroses.

"It's what the advertisement said," Kay reminded her.

And there was no denying *that*.

"All I want now is my gardener," the lady said.

"The milkman's boy would come," Gerald said. "I'm sure he would." Maybe not in the daytime, but evenings and weekends, Gerald was sure. It would be such a good chance to get the bicycle more quickly.

"Well — " the lady said, doubtfully, and then, "Well, that would be wonderful, if you'd tell him for me," because a boy who didn't know much would be better than one who did but never came at all.

"We'll go and tell him tomorrow," Kay promised.

It still wasn't quite over, she thought happily. There was the night watchman to tell that they'd got the scooter and the bicycle back; and the Rag and Bone boy to give the baker's message to; and the milkman's boy who was now the chandler's boy to give the money to and tell about the gardening job for when he wasn't working for the —

"What's a chandler?" Kay asked Gerald, because although Gerald wasn't any good at ideas, he knew words and what they meant.

"A dealer in candles," Gerald said, quick as a flash. "People didn't always have gas and electricity, they used candles instead. Chandlers sold other things as well — like soap and oil and paint and corn. My father says when that old shop comes down the name will disappear."

Kay hoped it wouldn't. It was a nice word, she thought. Next time her mother sent her shopping for soap, or oil, or paint, that's where she'd go.

Gerald threw a leg over his bicycle. It was almost too good to be true that he'd got his bike back again, and not really any the worse for its adventures — only the scratch on the handlebar, and if it hadn't been for that he might never have got it back at all.

"Let's race to the end of the road," Rory cried. Kay had already pushed off on her roller skates, keeping up with Gerald, but he didn't mind. When they got to the end of the road they'd be waiting for him.

About the Author

DOROTHY CLEWES is a favorite among young readers. She has a special talent for getting her characters in and out of trouble, in a way that is both believable and fun. Mrs. Clewes lives in Kent, England.